For Lentil, and all the adventures
that await you
- S. C.

For all my girlfriends who have kindness
in their heart and DIY in their soul!
- C. P.

tiger tales
5 River Road, Suite 128, Wilton, CT 06897
Published in the United States 2019
Originally published in Great Britain 2019
by Little Tiger Press Ltd.
Text by Suzanne Chiew
Text copyright © 2019 Little Tiger Press Ltd.
Illustrations copyright © 2019 Caroline Pedler
ISBN-13: 978-1-68010-149-2
ISBN-10: 1-68010-149-8
Printed in China
LTP/1800/2635/0219
10 9 8 7 6 5 4 3 2 1

For more insight and activities, visit us at www.tigertalesbooks.com

Badger AND THE Big ADVENTURE

by Suzanne Chiew   Illustrated by Caroline Pedler

tiger tales

One crisp fall afternoon, Badger sat in
his cozy home, knitting a brand-new scarf.
Suddenly, he heard noises outside.
"What's going on out there?" he wondered,
rushing to the door.

In the sunshine stood Hedgehog and Rabbit with
three little birds chirping noisily on the ground.
"Badger! What should we do?" cried Hedgehog.
"These poor birds have been separated from their flock!"
"They were flying south for the winter," explained Rabbit,
"when the youngest hurt her wing."

Badger picked up the littlest bird. "Oh, dear! That wing needs time to heal," he said. "Why don't you stay with me until you're strong enough to fly?"

"Thank you! Thank you!" tweeted the birds.

Winter arrived, bringing with it blankets of snow, but the three little birds stayed safe and warm inside Badger's house.

Every morning the birds sang Badger a happy song.

Each day was filled with laughter and cheer.

And every evening they read stories by the fire.

One morning, Badger woke up to find the birds singing more loudly than ever.

"Spring is here!" they chirped.

"And look! I can fly again!" peeped the littlest bird.

But after a short time in the air, she fluttered to the ground.

Later that day, Badger found her perched sadly by the window.

"Our flock will soon be passing on their way back home," she sniffed. "How will we join them if I can't fly very far?"

"Don't worry," smiled Badger. "Every problem has a solution!" And his eyes twinkled with a new idea.

The next day, Hedgehog and Rabbit came over
to hear all about Badger's plan.

"Ooh! What's that?" asked Rabbit as Badger
laid out his sketches.

"A flying machine," explained Badger. "Swift and
speedy to help us reach the flock!"

"Hooray!" cheered Rabbit and Hedgehog,
and they all got to work.

They measured . . .

and sawed . . .

and glued all day long.
"Many hands make
light work," sang Badger.
"We're almost finished!"

At sunrise, the friends pushed the flying machine
to the top of a hill.

"Quick, jump in!" yelled Badger as it started
rolling down the grassy slope. "Here we go!"

And with one last BUMP . . .

. . . the machine took to the skies.

"Wow!" gasped Hedgehog. "Flying
is incredible!"

"You can see everything from up here,"
beamed Rabbit. "Look—there's Mole's
house, and that's where Mouse lives!"

On they soared, over rivers and rolling hills.
Suddenly, the littlest bird began to chirp.

"Our flock!" she cried, spotting her friends
in the distance.

"Time to catch up with them!" declared
Badger, and they raced ahead.

"Where have you been?" cried the flock,
fluttering with joy. "We've been so worried!"

"My wing was hurt, but I'm better now,"
laughed the littlest bird. "And it's all
thanks to our new friends."

Soon it was time for
the flock to continue its
journey home.
"Safe travels!" waved Badger.
"We'll miss you!" twittered the
little birds. "Good-bye! Good-bye!"

"What a special day,"
cheered Hedgehog as
they started back home.

But suddenly, a crash of thunder made
the flying machine rattle and shake.
"Hold on tight!" warned Badger.
"I can't look!" gulped Rabbit.
Lightning lit up the sky as they
steered through the stormy clouds.
"Get ready for a bumpy landing!"
Badger hollered, and down they swooped.

At last the friends were safely on the ground.
"What an adventure!" said Rabbit. "But I'm
glad we're home."

Later on, Badger thought of the happy times he had shared with the little birds.

"I'm going to miss them," he sighed.

As the days passed, spring turned into summer, and bees buzzed happily all around. Badger kept busy in his garden, but every now and then, he would think of the little birds and smile.

Fall returned, bringing with it colorful leaves, golden afternoons, and a big surprise . . . .

"You're back!" cried Badger,
hearing a familiar chirpy song.
"Of course!" tweeted the birds.
"We have so much to tell you!"
And from that year on, when
the leaves began to fall, Badger
enjoyed a visit from his very
special friends.